The recipes in this book are intended
to be prepared under adult supervision.

This book
is dedicated to
my mother and father
and
Kristi Snyder

Henry Holt
and Company, Inc.
Publishers since 1866
115 West 18th Street, New York, New York 10011
Henry Holt is a registered trademark of Henry Holt and Company, Inc.
Copyright© 1995 by Olga Bravo. All rights reserved. Published in Canada
by Fitzhenry & Whiteside Ltd., 195 Allstate Parkway, Markham, Ontario L3R 4T8.
Library of Congress Cataloging-in-Publication Data
Bravo, Olga. Olga's Cup and Saucer/by Olga Bravo.
Summary: Through the summer months, Nickel Penny brings fresh
fruits and vegetables to the bakery next to her father's farm,
hoping to be allowed to help with the baking. Includes recipes.
[1. Bakers and bakeries—Fiction. [2. Baking—Fiction.] 1.Title
PZ7. B738401 1994 [E]—dc20   94-33823
ISBN 0-8050-3301-7/First edition—1995
The artist used watercolor and ink on Windsor & Newton paper.
Printed in the United States of America on acid-free paper.∞
1 3 5 7 9 10 8 6 4 2

Olga's cup and Saucer

OPEN

A Picture Book with Recipes by
OLga Bravo

Henry Holt and Company
New York

June

Early one June morning, before the sun has had a chance to peek over the horizon, Nickel Penny is awakened by the strong smells of brown sugar and cinnamon, bread baking, and strawberry corn muffins cooling. "They're open!"

Nickel Penny lives next to a bakery. It sits on the edge of a farm beside a roadside farm stand. The stand sells the farm's fresh fruits and vegetables and jellies and jams from summer to fall.

The bakery is called Olga's Cup and Saucer because it belongs to Olga and it is as tiny as a teacup.

Nickel Penny thinks of the people sitting outside eating pieces of fresh baked pie and sipping cups of tea as a welcome sign.

Nickel Penny wants to be a baker. She had been watching the bakers bake since the day she was born. She wants to be inside the kitchen with a big white hat and a clean white apron, near the warmth of the ovens, surrounded by the smells.

"Oh, look inside," says Nickel Penny.

"The bread is rising. The bowls of dough are like mountains. The sink is overflowing with pots and pans. And look at those muffins!"

Suddenly, knives stop chopping. Whisks stop beating.
It grows quiet inside the kitchen.

"Oh, pooh!" the bakers say. "We have run out of strawberries.
We can't make more muffins, and the line of customers will be
out the door!"

"That's it!" cries Nickel Penny. "If I pick the strawberries,
they're sure to let me in!"

And off she runs to find
the juiciest berries for Olga.

Strawberry Corn Muffins

Makes 18 muffins

2 cups cornmeal*
2 cups unbleached white flour
2/3 cup sugar
5 teaspoons baking powder
1/2 teaspoon salt

1 quart fresh strawberries, with
the stems picked off and
the berries cut into small pieces
2 cups plain yogurt
1/2 cup canola oil
2 large eggs, slightly beaten

*Use as good a quality cornmeal as you can find. Olga gets her cornmeal from a local gristmill.

1. Preheat oven to 350°.

2. Prepare a muffin tin by greasing with butter or using paper muffin liners.

3. In a large bowl, mix together the dry ingredients (cornmeal, flour, sugar, baking powder, and salt) using a wire whisk.

4. Add the strawberries, tossing gently to coat with flour mixture.

5. In a smaller bowl, whisk together the yogurt and canola oil.
   Add the slightly beaten eggs.

6. Add the yogurt mixture to the dry ingredients. Mix together with a wooden spoon until the dry ingredients are just barely wet. Do not overmix.

7. Scoop out muffin batter with a wooden spoon and fill muffin tin to the brim.

8. Bake 20 to 30 minutes.

July

Mr. Rooster the farmer is Nickel Penny's daddy.

Nickel Penny loves him very much. He takes her all over the farm on a special seat next to his on the tractor. He plants the corn, grows the herbs, and picks the zucchini that Olga uses for her muffins and cakes.

A-Z
Afternoon cake

(Apples, Carrots, Raisins, and Zucchini)

Serves 12

1/4 cup sugar
4 cups unbleached white flour
1-1/2 tablespoons cinnamon
1-1/2 tablespoons baking powder
1 teaspoon salt

1 cup flaked coconut
1 cup raisins
2 cups carrots (2 medium carrots), grated
2 cups zucchini (1 medium zucchini), grated
2 whole apples, grated

6 large eggs, slightly beaten
2 cups canola oil
1 teaspoon vanilla extract

1. Preheat oven to 375°.

2. In a large mixing bowl, whisk together the sugar, flour, cinnamon, baking powder, and salt.

3. Add the coconut, raisins, carrots, zucchini, and apples to the dry mixture.

4. In a smaller bowl, whisk together the eggs, canola oil, and vanilla extract.

5. Add the wet ingredients to the dry, mixing only until the dry are just slightly wet. Don't worry if the batter is lumpy; it is better to undermix than to overmix.

6. Grease a 13 x 9 x 2-inch pan.

7. Spread batter evenly in pan.

8. Bake for 40 to 45 minutes, or until fork comes out clean when cake is pricked. Cool on rack. Serve warm or at room temperature.

"Who will help me pick the blueberries?
Who will help me pick the peaches?
Who will help me gather all the baskets?"
asks Mr. Rooster in the middle of July.

"Not I," says the boy with the fishing pole resting on his shoulder, walking toward the pond.

"Not I," says the boy wandering into the field of flowers, with a book in his hands.

"Not I," says the boy lying in the shade of the tree, with his skunk cap pulled over his eyes.

"I will!" yells Nickel Penny. "I will help."

And when the blueberries and peaches are picked and the baskets gathered, Nickel Penny delivers them to Olga with the hope of helping her make the cobblers.

Blueberry Peach Cobbler

Makes 4 small individual cobblers

Biscuit Topping:

3 cups unbleached white flour
3 tablespoons sugar
1-1/2 tablespoons baking powder
3/4 teaspoon cream of tartar
1 teaspoon kosher salt

Zest of 1/2 lemon, minced (save inside of lemon for fruit filling)
3/4 cup vegetable shortening (Crisco)
3/4 cup milk
1 large egg, beaten

1. Preheat oven to 375°.

2. In a medium-size mixing bowl, combine the flour and sugar. Sift in baking powder, cream of tartar, and salt. Add the lemon zest and nutmeg. Whisk until blended.

3. Cut in the shortening to the flour mixture until it is the consistency of cornmeal. You can do this with your hands. Make a well in the center of the mixture.

4. In a small bowl, combine the milk with the beaten egg.

5. Make a well in the center of the shortening mixture. Add the liquid ingredients to the flour mixture and blend with a fork, using small strokes and being careful not to overmix. Set aside in the refrigerator as you prepare the fruit filling.

Fruit Filling:

3 ripe peaches
  (approximately 2 cups),
  skinned and pitted,
  cut into large wedges
1 pint blueberries (3 cups),
  washed and stems picked out
1 tablespoon fresh lemon juice

6 tablespoons sugar,
  adjusted according to
  sweetness of the fruits
3 tablespoons flour
1/4 teaspoon fresh nutmeg
3 tablespoons cold butter,
  cut up into small pieces

1. In a medium-size bowl, place prepared fruit. Sprinkle with lemon juice.

2. Add the sugar, flour, and nutmeg.

To assemble cobbler:

1. Place fruit mixture in 4 small individual pie tins or Pyrex baking cups. Top fruit mixture with pats of very cold butter.

2. Scoop out spoonfuls of biscuit batter with your fingers and gently place on top until all the fruit is covered.

3. Bake for 30 to 45 minutes until biscuit top has golden peaks and the fruit is bubbling below. Cool on a rack before serving.

August

August is very hot and dry. The cornfields behind Nickel Penny's house are tall and thick. The bees buzz around the raspberry bushes, which are full of red, plump, sticky fruit.

"I'm so thirsty," Nickel Penny says to Sugar, her cat. She stands in the middle of the raspberry bushes, where she was picking a pint of berries.

"Let's get some lemonade from Olga's."

Ginger Lemonade

Makes 1 (2-quart) pitcher

Lemons:

5 lemons, halved and squeezed
1-inch fresh gingerroot, skinned and roughly chopped
1/4 cup cold water

1. In a blender, puree the lemon juice with the gingerroot and water.

2. Pour through a strainer. Throw away the pulp and pour liquid into a pitcher.

Simple Syrup:

1 cup water
1/2 cup sugar

1. Bring water and sugar to a boil, stir, and transfer to a bowl in an ice bath (so as to cool quickly).

2. Add the simple syrup to the pitcher. Fill pitcher with water and/or ice. Adjust for desirable sweetness by adding more water.

Olga is very busy. Becky the pizza chef is out sick and the kitchen is a mess.

Flour flies through the air and lands on the tip of Olga's nose as she finishes the pizza dough.

Nickel Penny walks through the kitchen, holding her ice-cold lemonade in one hand and balancing the pint of raspberries in the other. Suddenly...

...Nickel Penny trips on a basket of tomatoes, and raspberries fly through the air.

Then she hears Olga exclaim, "Raspberry Pizza, what a great idea! Nickel Penny, you have become such a creative baker!"

Fresh Raspberry Pizza

Pizza Dough:

1 package dry, active yeast (1 tablespoon)
1 cup lukewarm water
2 tablespoons olive oil
2 cups unbleached white flour (plus 1/2 cup for kneading)
1/3 cup fresh ground cornmeal (plus 4 tablespoons to coat pans)
1 tablespoon orange zest, minced
pinch of salt

Raspberry Pizza Topping:

1 pint fresh raspberries
3 tablespoons sugar
1 teaspoon cinnamon
2 ounces bittersweet chocolate
4 tablespoons melted butter
1/2 cup sliced almonds
confectioner's sugar

To prepare dough:

1. In a medium-size bowl, add the lukewarm water to the yeast. Whisk together and set aside until yeast has dissolved or until white bubbles have formed on top. Stir in the olive oil, orange zest, and salt. Slowly add the flour and cornmeal until it is too sticky to stir.

2. Flour a small portion of a kitchen table and turn the dough onto it. Knead by lifting the sides of the dough and with the addition of flour, rolling and pushing down the dough until it is not sticky but smooth and elastic.

3. Brush the bowl with 1 teaspoon of olive oil and return the dough to it. Cover the bowl with a clean kitchen towel and place in a warm, draft-free spot until the dough has doubled in size (about 30 minutes).

4. After it has doubled in size, punch down the dough to let out the air. Turn out onto the floured surface and divide into 4 even pieces. Cover with the same kitchen towel and let the dough rise again for about 15 minutes.

5. Sprinkle the 4 tablespoons of cornmeal on 2 ungreased cookie sheets. Uncover the balls of dough. Working on a floured surface, push out each ball using your fingertips until you have a thin flat circle or any shape you like.

6. Preheat oven to 375°. Keep the sheet pans covered with a cloth and in a warm spot while preparing the topping.

To assemble pizza:

1. Transfer the raspberries to a bowl, picking out stems and leaves. Do not wash the berries. They are too delicate and will get soggy.

2. In a small bowl, mix together the cinnamon and sugar.

3. Chop chocolate into small pieces.

4. Uncover the sheet pans and brush dough with melted butter using a pastry brush. Sprinkle with cinnamon and sugar mixture. Dot with raspberries and sprinkle with chocolate pieces. Scatter the tops with almonds and drizzle with remaining butter.

5. Bake for 20 minutes, or until the chocolate has melted and the butter is bubbling. Dust with confectioner's sugar. Serve warm.

September

The first
Monday in September
is Labor Day, when the
summer season winds to an end.
The row of sunflowers that have grown
tall all summer have bowed their heavy
heads. Small orange pumpkins are growing in
the distant fields.

Olga and Nickel Penny and Mr. Rooster celebrate Labor Day with
all their friends at an outdoor feast. Zucchini pies are baked, corn
is shucked, tomatoes are sliced.

In between the tomato salad and zucchini pie, Nickel Penny, Olga's new baker, falls asleep, dreaming up new recipes for the next season.